"The Jasper family's heartwarming tales of adventure and fun will be sure to keep both boys and girls actively involved in re       This whole-some and timeless read-alo         ⁺o-twelve year olds will draw pare⁻              ⸻ether in a delightful readir

                                          ⸻ly Michael
                                          ⸻et 16 ghostwriter
                                          ⸻nor of *Crooked Lines*

"*Meet the Jaspers* ⸻    ⸻eartfelt collection of de-lightful experiences and lessons learned by a won-derful, loving family. It's a true picture of family values and love. Parents and children alike will relate to the real life experiences the Jaspers en-counter, the way they handle them and what they learn along the way about themselves, each other and life. It's touching and funny at the same time. How each member of the family relates to one another and works through their circumstances is a lesson in itself. The book is inspirational, funny, and moving. A wonderful read."

-Camille Kocsis
Speaker, Teacher, Master Success Coach and Author
Successful Living Seminars

# Meet the
# JASPERS

To Hal's Darling
Jean, à
Merry Christmas !
Love your family
Beth Strong

Published by Tate Publishing & Enterprises, LLC
127 E. Trade Center Terrace | Mustang, Oklahoma 73064 USA
1.888.361.9473 | www.tatepublishing.com

Tate Publishing is committed to excellence in the publishing industry. The company reflects the philosophy established by the founders, based on Psalm 68:11,
*"The Lord gave the word and great was the company of those who published it."*

Book design copyright © 2012 by Tate Publishing, LLC. All rights reserved.
*Cover and interior design by Elizabeth M. Hawkins*
*Illustrations by Julie Love Yarbor*

Published in the United States of America

ISBN: 978-1-62024-461-6
1. Juvenile Fiction / Action & Adventure / General
2. Fiction / Family Life
12.07.19

# Meet the
# JASPERS

## by Beth Strong

tate publishing
CHILDREN'S DIVISION

# Dedication

I would like to dedicate this book to my husband, Bryan. You are always such a source of support and encouragement to me in all that I do. I am so grateful that God gave us each other, and we are able to take this fantastic journey together.

I am also grateful for our own three little Jaspers who are not so little anymore: Jake, Emma, and Ben. You have been good sports about having your own childhood antics exposed and exaggerated. Thank you for making my life so full of joy and abundance.

# Acknowledgments

My Lord and Savior Jesus Christ—without You, we are nothing. I know that you are always with me in all that I do. Through You, all things are possible. You are leading me and guiding me on each path that I choose to take (Ephesians 2:8-10, 1 John 1:9, 2 Timothy 3:16-17).

My mom—you are my consultant, inspiration, and encourager. Thank you for gifting me with your love of books. As a child, I waited with anticipation to hear you read aloud at the breakfast table, on a car ride, around the campfire, and at bedtime. This is just one example of the many beautiful gifts of love you have given.

Matt Sprague and Mark Sprague—my brothers and fellow members of The Front Porch Band. Thank you for being an inspiration for some of the antics of the Jaspers. What an amazing way to grow up and I wouldn't change a thing.

Larry Flanders—my English teacher and friend. Thank you for believing and planting the seed. Your encouragement on a 7th grade essay started the dream. Excellent teachers are so valuable and have such great impact. Thank you.

My dear supporters and confidants— Camille Kocsis, Holly Michael, Amy Ridgely, Karen Sprague, Amy Ferguson, Shannon Sherwin, and Sandi Owens. Thank you for your love and friendship.

# Table of Contents

# Weekend Campout

"You really mean it?" Katie Jasper asked. "It's really time to go?"

Finally, the big weekend had arrived. This was the time the whole family had waited for. The Jaspers were going camping.

Katie, who was six, had packed her bag two days ago, when Dad broke the news that they were going camping. They were off to Cedar Lake for a weekend of fun and sun with their beloved pop-up travel trailer. It would be fantastic. Katie didn't even care about the mosquito bites she would most likely be covered in. Every time they camped, mosquitoes and black flies seemed to find Katie. Mom said it was because she tasted so sweet.

"What have you got in there?" Jason asked. Jason was Katie's big brother. "That backpack weighs a ton."

Jason was the oldest child in the Jasper family and a big nine-year-old at that. Katie noticed that he was always the tallest in his class at school. Jason stood in the back row for music programs every year.

"I've got three swimsuits, four pairs of shorts, three t-shirts, two pairs of pants, socks, undies, and two pairs of pajamas for hot and cold weather. Oh yeah. My robe too," Katie replied. She failed to mention her special blankie, her Little Bear books, her pink spongy hair curlers, and Puffy— her best stuffed animal.

# Meet the Jaspers

"Jeepers. What's all that for? I'm bringing my swim trunks and a clean t-shirt just in case," commented Jason.

"You just never know what you're gonna need," Katie answered as her long, blonde hair caught sunshine from the window.

"Kids," Mom called up the stairs in her sing-songy voice. "Let's get going. Bring your bags down, and make sure you use the bathroom before we leave."

"I don't have to go," answered Ben, who was three and a half and like it or not, he was Katie and Jason's little brother.

"Just try, please," said Mom as she checked the contents of Ben's backpack. "Benny, where did the clean clothes go that we packed in your bag last night?"

"I needed more room for my tractor and digger," Ben answered, as if it made perfect sense.

"Well, sweetie, you can't wear a bulldozer if you get wet from fishing," Mom said with a smile as she pointed to the toys in his bag.

Sometimes Katie thought that she and Jason should receive some special attention since they were generally well behaved and were thoughtful toward others. However, Benny often found a way to become the center of attention with his smiling eyes, round belly, and cowlick smack dab in the middle of his forehead.

Jason was going into the fourth grade, studied hard, and loved most sports. When school started in the fall, Katie was going to be a first-grader. Katie was in the middle of the two boys. Katie was a reader already when she graduated from kindergarten in the spring. Dad said she was a math whiz too.

The minivan was packed full. There was a cooler between Jason's legs and sleeping bags stacked underneath Katie and Ben's feet. Fishing poles were tucked in at their sides, and beach towels were stuffed in at the ceiling. There was scarcely room for Woody, their family dog.

"Are we ready?" Dad asked.

"Yes," the kids all chorused, which caused Woody to give an understanding bark.

"All righty then. Let's go," Dad said as he rubbed his hands together excitedly.

The ride to Cedar Lake seemed to take forever.

"Are we there yet?" asked Katie.

"Sweetie, it's only a forty-five-minute drive, and we've been driving for fifteen minutes. We're getting closer," Dad answered.

The gravel road to the campground was lined with trees that seemed to drape over the top of the road and make a canopy cover. They turned the last corner and stopped at the registration gate, where they could finally see Cedar Lake. It was a small, inland lake with a sandy bottom and beach just right for playing. There was also a more isolated area with shrubs and reeds that helped with fishing.

It was a glorious blue-sky day, and the water had a bluish-green hue to it. Trees surrounded the campground and divided each campsite. That's why the Jaspers picked the Cedar Lake Campground—because they liked to get away from it all. Katie heard her parents talking about how *roughing it* was good for kids. Besides, outdoor toilets were fun; no loud flushing noise. Since there wasn't electricity, Katie got to watch her parents cook on the propane stove and on the charcoal grill. She also loved to help wash the dishes outside on the picnic table with a dishpan. They had to warm the dishwater in a pan on the propane stove since there wasn't any hot running water at this campground. Katie noticed how it was more fun to wash camping dishes than the ones at home. One of Katie's favorite things was to hear a bedtime story read to her by the light of a lantern. She could hardly wait for the fun to begin.

"Let's look for a campsite. Keep your eyes peeled," Dad said.

"Isn't that going to hurt, Dad?" Jason asked.

"What, son?"

"Peeling our eyeballs." Jason snorted.

"Okay then, Mr. Funny Man. What I meant was, let's be on the *lookout* for a campsite," Dad responded with a smile.

As they drove around to the backside of the campground, they all knew they had found the perfect campsite.

"This site is the one. It's right on the water with those thick trees between our site and the next-door neighbors," noticed Dad. "Besides, the outdoor toilets are only fifty feet away."

"There's a metal ring for our campfire," Katie observed. She also noticed the brown, wooden picnic table.

Dad began to back the trailer into the spot while Mom used hand signals to guide him in. Soon they were turning the hand crank to raise the roof of the trailer and push out the pop-out wings. Then they had to level the camper to make sure that one end wasn't higher than the other.

"Hey, kids, why don't you go gather some small kindling wood to start our campfire tonight," Mom suggested. "Make sure you stay right by the campsite. Once we're all set up we can have lunch."

"Did you bring the *kabloney*, Mom?" asked Ben.

"Of course I brought the bologna, sweet-ie," Mom said as she bent down to kiss Ben-ny on the nose. "I brought the ketchup too."

Ben loved "keputch" and "kabloney"

sandwiches almost as much as he loved to dress up in his superhero costumes. Katie wasn't sure why Ben replaced the *k* sound at the beginning of some words.

The trio went off in search of firewood for the evening near their site.

"We better make sure we find plenty of kindling to help get the fire started," Jason offered.

Ben started to gather huge logs as big as he could drag. He groaned and muttered as he tried to pull the big chunks back to the fire pit. Beads of sweat began to form on the little boy's face.

"*Kindling* is the little branches and birch bark that help *start* the fire, Benny," Jason offered helpfully.

"Oh. Now we have big logs," Ben said as his cheeks turned even redder.

"Kids! Lunch!" Mom sang out through the trees.

They all inhaled their food as they had worked up quite an appetite.

"My *kaputch*-and-*kabloney* sandwich was *kalicious*, Mommy," said Ben.

"I'm glad you enjoyed your lunch, guys," said Mom.

"Maybe it's time for us to get ready to go for a swim," Dad said.

"Wahoo!" exclaimed the three kids in unison.

This was one of the best parts of camping: the swimming part.

Mom made sure to give them a little extra time to let their food digest before they got into the water. They gathered up their goggles, snorkels, fins, inner tubes, and boogie boards. They also got sunscreen spread over every square inch of their bodies.

A big sand dune hill led down to the water. They ran fast down the hill, right into the water. After the sixteenth try, they were tired. Then they pulled out their beach toys from the bag. The boys snorkeled in the shallow water while Katie dug in the sand. Soon, all three were involved in building a nine-castle compound surrounded by a moat. The hours drifted away as they played and Dad and Mom relaxed in the sand. Woody had fun swimming and chasing the tennis ball.

"Katie, you have a bug on your *kikini*," Ben noticed.

"Ah! Get off my bikini, you silly old bug," Katie said as she swished the air around her swimsuit. Katie hated bugs. "Shoo. Go away."

Katie loved days like this where they could just play on and on without thinking about the clock, soccer practice, or chores. The Jaspers spent all of their time together on camping trips.

Katie saw the sun start to sink in the sky. She knew that the five-minute warning was coming soon from her parents. Besides, Katie could hear her belly growling. She hated to ask for food because she knew her parents would say it was time to pack up.

This had been so much fun. She hated to see it end.

"What was that sound, Katie?" Jason asked as they dug in the sand next to each other.

"I think that's my stomach growling. I'm *starvated*," Katie answered quietly.

"I'm really hungry too," Jason responded as they both began to dream about how great the grilled hamburger would taste with the corn on the cob and fried potatoes.

So it was no surprise when Dad said, "We better pack it in if we're going to get the coals lit for the grill."

They sadly gathered up their things reluctantly and walked slowly back up the sand dune hill that led back to their campsite.

# Meet the Jaspers

Before they knew it, they could smell the burgers grilling and the sweet corn simmering.

*There's nothing better than a delicious meal cooked outside after a fun day with your family,* Katie thought. She was really looking forward to sleeping in the camper too.

"Who wants cheese on their burger?" Dad asked.

"I do," answered Ben, "No fried *kotatoes* please."

After dinner, the Jaspers enjoyed a nice big campfire with all of the kindling and big logs they had gathered. They roasted marshmallows and put them on a honey graham cracker with a chocolate candy bar to make s'mores.

"These really are *kalicious*," said Jason.

Ben's extra *k*'s were starting to rub off on him now.

Mom and Dad started to tell a few funny

stories around the campfire. Most of them were about silly things they did when they were kids.

"When I was about Katie's age, I found a nest of baby field mice when I was out playing one afternoon," said Mom. "I carried the little pink, bald babies home in my pocket to show my brother to try to impress him. When Grandma asked if I had washed my hands for dinner, I said yes. I felt terrible about it. It feels awful to tell a lie even if no one finds out about it. Of course, Grandma *did* find out when she found those poor baby mice in my pocket in the laundry hamper. Grandma hated mice."

Mom's story got interrupted by Katie's scream.

Suddenly, a huge, black, furry creature ambled by the edge of their campsite. It was a bear.

"Everybody, stay calm," Dad whispered

as the bear was walking toward their picnic table. "Don't anybody move."

Mom scooped up Benny in her arms, and Dad held Katie. Katie could feel her heart pound in her chest at the sight of this huge, black bear. She held onto her dad extra tight.

The bear made a big swipe with his paw and knocked the bag of marshmallows and the graham crackers to the ground. He then picked the food up in his mouth and lumbered off through the trees to the next campsite.

The park ranger had warned them that they might meet up with a bear. He said it was best to stay back and be still. They only wanted food and *probably* wouldn't hurt you.

"Is everybody okay?" Mom asked.

"I think so," Jason answered as his heartbeat started to slow down. "That thing was huge."

Katie started to whimper once she realized what had just happened.

"You guys did great doing just what we said," Dad complimented. "Don't panic if you see a bear. Never try to outrun a bear because you won't win."

"I can run really fast," Ben said.

"Bears can run faster than humans, and they can climb trees too. It's best to stay calm and don't make them angry. That bear just wanted our food anyway. He was a campground bear that was used to humans. The bear knew we'd have some good bedtime snacks to eat."

"On that note, I think that it is time for the Jaspers to hit the hay," Mom said. "You guys will need some sleep if we're going to catch some fish in the morning."

"Is it safe? I'm scared that bear will try to get in our camper while we're asleep," Katie said.

"Don't worry, honey. He already got his bedtime snack, like you. Now he's ready for bed just like you are," Mom offered.

# Meet the Jaspers

"If he comes back, could you make him a *kaputch*-and-*kabloney* sandwich, Mom?" Ben asked. "He oughta like that."

"Let's just wash our dirty hands and feet off a bit before we get our pajamas on," Mom said as she handed out the baby wipes.

Katie liked it when she didn't have to take a bath. This was another reason she thought camping was fun. Everyone snuggled into their sleeping bags. Katie was so tired from her big day that she didn't have the energy to worry about the bear anymore and fell fast asleep.

The next thing Katie knew, she was waking up with the smell of coffee brewing and bacon sizzling. The sky was a little cloudy as she peeked through the canvas zipper opening that was a window in their camper.

The others began to stir as the good

breakfast smells filled the air. Benny's hair seemed to be confused and heading in several different directions because of his cowlicks. The barber once counted seven cowlicks in his hair and found Ben's hair very hard to cut.

"Come here, Ben," Mom said as she reached for him.

"I've got the perfect fishing spot all figured out," Dad said.

After breakfast was eaten and cleaned up, they were on their way to catch some fish. All five of the Jaspers were ready to go. Woody stayed at the campsite. Katie knew that Jason was really excited. He had yet to catch his first fish of the summer. He was trying to be patient, but it was hard.

The Jaspers hiked through the swamp and bushes to get to one of Dad's tried-and-true fishing spots. Dad was using some pretty feisty nightcrawlers as bait. They were chub-

by and full of life and did not willingly get fastened to the end of the hook. Soon they were tossing their lines into the fast-moving stream, which flowed into Cedar Lake.

It didn't take Ben long to get the first bite. He saw the red-and-white bobber sink below the surface of the water to signal that something was nibbling at his worm.

"Ben, I think you've got a bite," Dad said. "Let me help you set the hook."

Dad pulled back on the fishing pole slightly and began to reel. Then he handed the pole over to Ben so he could land his own fish. Ben began to turn the handle of the reel.

"This must be a whopper," Ben said as he stopped to rest.

"Keep it up, son. You're doing great," Dad said.

Soon the little bullhead was on the bank of the stream.

"Great job, Ben!" Mom cheered. "Let

me get a picture of you holding the first fish you ever caught."

Katie noticed a funny look on Jason's face. A little bit of jealousy burned in Jason's stomach.

"Why is he so lucky?" Jason said. "He's only three, and he caught a fish."

Before too long, Katie's bobber started to jump, and her little bell began to ring on the end of her pink Barbie fishing pole, signaling that another fish was on.

"Daddy! Help!" Katie cried. "I don't know what to do."

Ben grabbed her pole, set the hook, and began to reel in the fish.

"I think we've got quite a little fisherman on our hands here, Mom," said Dad. "What do you think?"

"Benny, why don't you let Katie try to reel it in the rest of the way since it is her Barbie pole," offered Mom.

"Here, Katie," said Ben. "This is fun."

"Yeah, it's fun if you catch fish," complained Jason. "I wouldn't know about that."

"Hey, Buddy," said Dad. "Why don't you ease up a little bit? I know it's hard to watch the others catch fish, but your time will come."

"I know, Dad, but they just seem so lucky," said Jason.

"When it comes to fishing, you've got to be patient," Dad advised. "You just never know when the big fish will come along."

With that, Ben's bobber took another dive as he began to reel in yet another bullhead.

"Look at my *bullfish*, Dad!" Ben said excitedly.

Jason rolled his eyes, as he was on the verge of tears.

"Good job, Ben," Dad encouraged.

"Good job, Ben," Jason repeated gloomily.

Just then, Mom got a bite at the same time Katie's bell began to ring.

# Meet the Jaspers

"These fish must be real hungry," said Mom as the two began to reel theirs in.

"Jason, do you want to use my pole for a change?" Katie offered helpfully.

"No. I wouldn't be caught dead using a Barbie fishing pole. Even if we are in the middle of nowhere," Jason said.

"Well, I think I've caught enough for today," said Katie. "Can I pick flowers?"

"Sure, honey. Just stay close to where I can see you," Mom said. "Why don't you look for a milkweed plant. Maybe you'll find a caterpillar or even a chrysalis getting ready to turn into a butterfly."

The sky was slightly overcast with a light summer breeze. It would be fall soon, and they would be back to school before they knew it, so Jason knew he better enjoy this time even if he couldn't seem to catch a fish to save his life.

Meanwhile, Katie was in search of

milkweed pods that the monarch caterpillar liked to feed on. Katie thought it was so much fun to find one and keep it in a coffee can with holes poked in the lid. This way she could watch the change take place. The caterpillar would soon form its chrysalis and then hatch into a beautiful orange-and-black monarch butterfly.

"Maybe if I look over by those trees, I could find one," Katie said to herself. "The trail is right here, so I won't get lost."

Katie found many daisies and dandelions. She knew not to pick wildflowers. They were meant to stay in nature. As soon as she looked up from her search, she realized that there was a big open area and two foot trails to choose from. Which one had she come from? Nothing looked familiar and the more she walked around, the more confused she got. Fear stabbed Katie's stomach and spread through her whole body. What was she thinking? Mom had told her to stay close, but she figured she could find her way. The more Katie wandered, the more scared she got. This forest was huge.

She started to cry out, "Daddy, Mommy, where are you?" Tears began to stream down her face. What if the bear came back?

Back at the stream, Ben was preparing to reel in yet another fish when Mom asked, "Where's Katie?"

"She's just at the top of that little hill over there," Dad pointed.

"No, she isn't," Mom replied, her voice sounding nervous. "Katie!" Mom called in a sing-songy tone.

There was no answer. Meanwhile, Mom and Dad frantically began looking for their little girl and called her name. Mom stayed with Ben so they wouldn't have two lost children. Jason was feeling guilty for being impatient with his little sister's luck with fishing.

Then a rhyme popped into Katie's head. Katie lost her mother at Mega Mart when they were shopping one time, and Mom taught her:

> If you're lost,
> Just stand still,
> Call for a grown-up,
> And wait until.

Katie stopped in her tracks. She kept calling out over and over again. She stayed right in the same spot and didn't feel quite so afraid once she remembered what to do.

Katie listened hard because she thought she heard her name being called. Yes, she heard her dad's voice calling, "Katie! Katie!"

"Daddy! I hear you! I'm here, Daddy!" called Katie.

Soon, she could see her dad jogging up over the hill. Katie opened her arms and ran toward him. Now she was crying happy tears as she wrapped her arms around his strong neck. He scooped her up and held her. Katie rubbed her tearstained face into her dad's chest and breathed a sigh of relief.

"You gave us quite a little scare, sweet pea. Where did you go?" Dad asked.

"I was looking for flowers *and* monarch caterpillars, but I couldn't find any, and then I couldn't find the right path, and then I got really scared," Katie said as she cried some more.

"Well, I've got you now, but don't do that again," Dad said as he gave her another hug. "You scared us to pieces. Let's go let Mom know that you're all right."

"They made their way back to the stream where they had been fishing just twenty minutes ago.

"Oh, Katie, we are so glad to see you," said Mom. "Are you okay?"

"I'm fine, Mommy," Katie answered. "But I remembered what you told me to do after *you* got lost at Mega Mart that one time." Then Katie recited the poem for her mother.

> If you're lost,
> Just stand still,
> Call for a grown-up,
> And wait until.

"That was the right thing to do. Always stop and wait for the grown-up to find you. If we're both moving, it's harder for us to find each other. Now what could we do to prevent this from happening again?" Mom asked.

"You told me to look for milkweed, Mommy," answered Katie.

"And I asked you to stay where I could see you," Mom finished.

"I know, Mommy. I'm sorry," Katie apologized.

# Meet the Jaspers

"It's okay, and I forgive you. Just please do what you're told. All right?" Mom said as she hugged Katie again.

"Can I have a hug?" asked Ben.

"Oh, sure. How about a group hug?" Dad offered.

"Do I have to? Because this is kind of dorky," Jason answered.

Just as Jason was getting ready to join his family, he saw his orange-and-yellow bobber sink underwater. With all of the commotion, Jason had left his line in the stream.

"Quick! I've got a bite."

Jason set the hook and began to reel. It felt big, but it was hard to tell because he had nothing to compare it to. He yanked and pulled and he reeled until his arms burned.

"I better get the net," Dad said. "This could be a real whopper."

And it was. Jason landed a fourteen-inch brook trout.

"That's one of the prettiest ones I've ever seen. Way to go, Jason!"

Jason was elated. *It was worth the wait,* he thought, *because this is an awesome fish.*

Mom took Jason's picture at the bank of the stream as he was holding his fish proudly.

"I don't know about you guys, but I think it's time to go get some lunch," Mom said.

"All of this excitement has made me famished," Dad said.

"We might have to go back home just to rest up from *this* weekend campout," said Mom with a smile.

# Street Hockey Extravaganza

"Car!" yelled Katie at the top of her lungs.

The kids playing in the street moved off to the edge where the car could pass by them safely. There was a street hockey extravaganza going on at Gardener Loop.

"Game on!" called Jason as all seven of the neighborhood kids flooded back into the street after the car had passed. Since this was a very quiet, dead-end street, the neighborhood kids could get away with skateboarding, scootering, rollerblading, biking, and all sorts of playing. The only people driving by their hockey game lived on the street.

Suddenly, Ben came running out of the Jaspers' garage with his small, red plastic hockey stick flailing in the air.

"Aah! *Geromino*! I'm here. I'm ready to play now," called Ben.

Mom had assured Katie that Ben was normal, but she still had her doubts. Ben didn't seem very normal at all. Ben was dressed up in his favorite Halloween costume, and it wasn't even close to Halloween yet. The costume consisted of a black cloth Batman mask and a cape floating behind him as he ran. Ben's round belly was covered by gray foam rubber from the costume. Now the costume made him look like he had rock-hard stomach muscles of the caped crusader.

# Meet the Jaspers

"Is the game still on?" asked Zack, who lived just up the street.

"Yeah. Just because my little brother is here doesn't mean we have to stop playing," answered Jason. "Game still on!"

Ben joined the two teams out in the middle of the street and began to run around, trying to hit the puck. He did manage to put his neon-green bike helmet on top of his head while still wearing his Batman face mask. He also wore his Velcro strap Batman sneakers that he could fasten all by himself. Thank goodness Ben didn't attempt roller blades today. As the puck received a slap shot and missed the net, it skittered off down the street, and everyone else was too tired to chase it.

"That's yours, Benny," Jason called.

"I'll get it!" Ben yelled in a husky voice as he gladly chased after the puck to give the others a much needed rest. Once he retrieved the puck though, he did not want to give it up. There was power in keeping the puck.

"Come on, Ben," pleaded Jason.

"No. I don't want to," Ben said with a twinkle in his eye.

"Hand me the puck and I'll give you a million dollars," offered Jason.

"Okay," said Ben as he reluctantly gave back the orange street puck. "Where's the money?"

"I'll give it to you later, Benny," answered Jason. "Game on!"

Street hockey was a real big deal on Gardener Loop, and when Cody said he couldn't be team captain anymore, Jason's heart secretly soared.

*Maybe I could take his place,* Jason thought. *Every team needs a captain.*

There was so much to organize and so much to be done if Jason was to take over. It really made sense since he had helped get the teams going originally anyway. Jason gathered his courage to ask the big question.

"Hey, Zack," Jason tried to ask casually, "what do you think about me taking Cody's place as team captain?"

"I don't care. I just know I don't want to be in charge anymore," answered Zack.

"Let's ask Bobby to see if he cares," said Jason.

Before he knew it, Jason had gotten himself elected as the new team captain of the neighborhood street hockey team. What an honor.

"Now the first thing we want to do is to have tryouts and then make a schedule of practices and games," said Jason as the ideas were spinning in his mind.

Jason ran into the house and rifled through a stack of books and papers, wildly searching for an old clipboard. Then, as he rearranged the junk drawer in his desk, he found a silver whistle he got from the dollar store.

"Who wants to try out for the team first?" asked Jason. "If we hurry, we can get two of you done before suppertime."

"Why do we need to try out?" asked Zack. "We're already *on* the team."

"Because this is what real teams do," responded Jason.

Jason organized his paper on the clipboard to critique the offense, defense, stick-handling skills, and slap shot of the athlete. Zack went first and felt great about his tryout.

Jason wrote on the clipboard and showed the result of his tryout. It read:

Zack
Offense/Good
Defense/Fair
Stick handling/Poor
Slap shot/Fair

# Meet the Jaspers

"Jeepers," Zack said as his face burned with embarrassment. "Am I that bad?"

"Bobby, you're next," said Jason.

Bobby also felt like he made a good showing of his skills during his tryout. His tryout sheet read:

Bobby
Offense/Fair
Defense/Good
Stick handling/Fair
Slap shot/Poor

Bobby also felt a pang of anxiety in his stomach.

"Hey, you guys did a good job," offered Jason. "Let's pick up with the rest of the tryouts tomorrow since it's time to go in for dinner and all." Jason kept thinking about how exciting it was to be the team captain. He felt so powerful and important.

"Yeah, sure," said the other boys disappointedly. "See you tomorrow."

Jason's excitement was bubbling over due to his newly appointed duty. It showed as they walked in the house together for dinner.

"Mom, where is the memo board that we used to write phone messages on?" asked Jason.

"I'm sure that it's in the garage somewhere, sweetie," Mom replied. "Check in the box marked 'dog toys and deer antlers.' But let's eat first. Okay? Wash up and help me set the table, please. Dad will be home in a few minutes."

"I would, Mom, but I've got so much to do before we finish hockey tryouts tomorrow. I have to start the team letter *and* make a practice and game schedule," said Jason.

"I'm so glad this is all working out for you, Jason, but it'll keep until after dinner," said Mom.

# Meet the Jaspers

Finally, after the table was cleared and the kitchen cleaned up, Jason could get on with the important business at hand. He began to write the letter for his new teammates.

Congratulations!
　　Welcome to the team. I'm very glad that you made the team. We will begin the following practice schedule next week.
　　Monday: 3:00-4:00
　　Tuesday: 4:00-6:00
　　Wednesday: 3:00-4:00
　　Friday: 3:00-4:00
　　All games Saturday: 4:00-6:00
　　*If you miss a practice, you will have to sit out the first half of the game. I'm looking forward to working with you.

Sincerely,
Jason Jasper
Team Captain

As Jason tried to fall asleep that night, his mind continued to plan how the rest of the tryouts would go tomorrow and how he would hand out the team letter to those who made it. They would have to name their team too. He had always thought that the Rangers would make a good name. Yeah, that was a great idea! Surely everyone would like that. It wasn't easy, but finally he fell asleep.

The next day, the tryouts continued as before. Soon all were completed. Jason began to hand out the welcome letter that included the schedule. His hand was tired because he had to write out six copies of the letter.

"Man, Jason," complained Zack," I can't make all of those practices. I know that I already have Cub Scouts on Tuesdays, and my sister has soccer on Wednesday."

"Yeah, we have baseball on Fridays too,"

said Bobby. "I guess we'll be missing the first half of the game Saturday."

Jason felt his face begin to burn. He realized that his own sister Katie had soccer starting soon, and he would probably miss hockey practice himself just to go to her practice. Mom said he wasn't old enough to be left home alone yet. Why hadn't he thought of that? He had remembered that he had his own baseball practice on Thursday and had purposefully not scheduled any practice on that day so he wouldn't miss anything.

"I've got to get something. I'll be right back," Jason called as he ran in to the house to think for a minute.

"Who put him in charge?" asked Bobby.

"We did," Zack replied, "Unfortunately, we've created a monster."

"Well, I think we need to give *him* a try-out and a bunch of low marks on his score-card," Bobby said angrily.

# Meet the Jaspers

"And then make up a practice schedule without asking anyone when they can come. Street hockey isn't even fun anymore," replied Zack.

Jason came out of the house with his whistle around his neck and his clipboard. "I figured we could use a few practice drills and we could work out our scheduling difficulties later," Jason said as he tested his stopwatch for accuracy.

Bobby and Zack rolled their eyes and fell into line as they were told.

"Is there a problem?" Jason asked. "I'm just trying to train you guys to be the best neighborhood street hockey team that we can possibly be."

"That's just it, Jason. It's not fun anymore. What happened to our team?" asked Zack. "I don't think I want to play anymore."

"Me either," said Bobby as Jason's two best buddies turned and walked up the street.

*What just happened here?* Jason asked himself as he turned away and moseyed up his driveway, his eyes welling up with tears.

"I thought you guys were having practice," said Dad while he was sharpening the lawnmower blade at his garage workbench.

"So did I," said Jason. "I guess the guys just couldn't take the pressure of organized street hockey."

"What do you mean, Jason?" Dad asked. "It seemed like you were having such a good time."

"Well, I worked so hard getting everything all organized, and the guys all got mad at me. I wrote a letter and made up a schedule."

"Why don't you show me the letter," Dad suggested. "Maybe that will help me understand."

Jason quickly fetched the letter with the schedule that he had worked so hard on.

"It's hard to be in charge, isn't it, Jason?" Dad asked as his face turned into a smile.

"Yeah. I did all the work to help the team be more professional, and they all got mad at me."

"How about we try to figure this out together."

"Sure, Dad. That would be great," Jason said with a little relieved smile.

"Let me ask you a question. Why don't you think about how you felt when Cody was the team captain? Did you like it?"

Jason thought about it a while and answered, "It was really fun. We just played and had a good time."

"How does it feel being on the team now, Jason?"

"Not so good. The team just walked away up the street."

"Do you like being the captain?" Dad kept asking so many questions.

"I really like to get everybody on a schedule and be organized. Being in charge was fun until everybody got mad and walked off."

"How do you think the others felt with your leadership style as team captain, buddy?"

"Not so good."

"Just think about how you'd like to be treated, and there is your answer. Just take some time to think about it, Jason. You'll know what to do," Dad suggested.

"Can't you just help me fix this with the guys, Dad? That would be so much easier."

"You can do this, Jason. Just remember that this is a neighborhood team and not a city league," Dad said with a smile as he returned to sharpening the blade.

Jason thought quietly to himself and then felt the answer come to him. He ran down the street to Zach's house. Jason nervously rang the door bell.

"Hey, Zach, can I talk to you about practice and stuff?" Jason shyly asked.

"Yeah. Sure. Are you adding more to the schedule?" Zach asked.

"No. Let's go see the others. I think they're outside now," Jason suggested.

They jogged down the street together, catching up with the guys outside who were practicing their 180's near the edge of the street on their skateboards.

"Hey guys. Wait up," Jason said as he swallowed hard and tried to get up his courage. "There's something I wanted to talk to you about. Sorry things got a little out of control with the whistle and the schedule and all. I was just wishing we could be more professional like the city leagues. Do you want to find a better schedule that works for everybody? I don't think we should sit out the first half of the game if anybody misses a practice either. Since this is a neighborhood team and not a city league, maybe things need to stay a little more relaxed. What do you think?"

"That sounds good," Zach answered excitedly. "I know you like to organize stuff. Sometimes you can't help it."

Jason answered with a smile, "I know it is how God made me, but I'll try to relax a little."

"Zack, don't you think it's about time for Jason to have his tryout now?" asked Bobby.

"I'll get the clipboard," said Zack.

"That sounds good," Jason answered, but he knew what he really needed to do. "No, that's okay. I'll go get it. Do you want the whistle too?" Jason asked with a giggle, trying to make a little fun of himself.

# Swimming Lesson
# Spectacular

"Do we have to go?" Jason complained to his mother.

"Miss Betty has been giving swimming lessons for over fifty years. She's an expert, and she's the best," said Mom. "That's why we're going to take lessons from her."

"But I already know how to swim," Jason said.

"But you keep learning every year, and you fine tune your skills," Mom offered.

"I know. I just don't want to give up my free time to go there with a bunch of little kids," Jason said. "How old is she anyway? Fifty years is a long time to give swimming lessons."

"Well, I heard that she started giving lessons when she was seventeen, so I would guess she's in her late sixties, but that's not polite to ask how old a lady is. Besides, you might even make a new friend."

"I doubt it."

"Well, get your suit on, and we'll make it fun," said Mom. "Katie! Benny! It's time for swimming lessons."

"Where's your *kikini*, Katie?" asked Benny as he entered the room.

"I just wanted to wear this one. It's more

swim lessony, don't you think?" asked Katie. She had on a bright-pink one-piece halter suit with purple flowers printed on it. It had a matching cover-up skirt.

"You look very ready for lessons," complimented Mom as they loaded into the van.

"Tell me again why we're going to Miss Betty?" asked Katie.

"Well, I know that you got great lessons at the city pool for the last few years, but we've been on Miss Betty's waiting list for three years, and she finally gave us a call that she had a cancellation of a family of three, so we're in," Mrs. Jasper said all in one breath as she smiled. "Even I took lessons from Miss Betty when I was a kid. In fact, Aunt Caroline, Grandma Peterson's baby sister, took lessons from her."

"No way, Mom," argued Jason.

"Way, Jason. She was one of Miss Betty's first students," teased Mom.

"Wow. That is old," offered Katie.

"Rather than concerning ourselves with how old Miss Betty is, let's think about how much fun we're going to have. Okay?" Mom said as they pulled up to the old, white-clapboard-sided country home.

Katie noticed shade trees everywhere she looked in the big yard. The in-ground pool was in the back of the yard, and Miss Betty was already gathering up students and breaking them up into groups.

Mom hadn't done enough to prepare the Jasper children for what they were about to see. Miss Betty was nearly six feet tall, which is pretty tall for a woman. She had wild, curly hair that had been dyed black to cover up the gray. She was very tan and very wrinkly from all of her years in the sun. Even though her skin looked old, her arms and legs looked like pure muscle. In fact, she looked like she could beat Katie's dad in a wrestling match. She wore a blue Speedo racing suit. It was the kind that the kids on the swim team wore.

"Hey, Susan. These must be your kiddos. Aren't they precious? I can't wait to get them in the water," Miss Betty said in a scratchy, raspy voice.

"Hi, Miss uh...Hi, Betty," Mom corrected herself.

Katie thought her mother sounded flustered and confused.

"It's so good to be here. Thanks for letting us squeeze in."

Ben just stood there in awe with his mouth hanging open. He wasn't quite sure what to do, so he just stood and stared at Miss Betty and her unique appearance.

"C'mon, kids. Let's head for the pool," said Mom.

"I'm not going in there," Ben whispered. "She's scary."

"Well, let's just go down closer to the pool and see what's going on," Mom said.

"Mom, are you trying to trick me?" Ben clung to the fence that surrounded the pool.

"He's fine, Susan. Now you go and sit in those chairs under the shade trees and relax a while. You've earned it," the swim teacher said as she pointed at the yard.

Mom turned and headed for the trees, secretly hoping her children wouldn't be afraid of Miss Betty. All she had considered was what a great swim teacher Miss Betty was and how badly she wanted her kids to have the instructor she had. Now Mom was embarrassed because Ben wouldn't get in the water and was bound to say something very impolite to his teacher.

"Benny, you just come in when you're ready. We'll just be over here in the shallow water, having fun with these other kids," said Miss Betty, and then she began to ignore Ben.

Katie and Jason were playing and splashing with the other three older kids while Miss Betty was talking to Ben's group. His group had four kids in it, counting Ben. Miss Betty had a helper to watch the other group. Ben was still holding on to the silver chain-link fence.

"Benny, why don't you just come over here and sit on the edge and dip your toes in? You don't have to get in or anything," Miss Betty coaxed.

Mom began to visit with the two other moms that were sitting in the shade. She looked apologetically to the others, and she was trying to figure out how to get Ben to go in the water. Then she looked toward the water and saw Ben sitting on the side of the pool with his legs dangling in up to his knees.

"How does she do it?" Mom asked with a sound of relief in her voice.

"I would imagine that she knows all of the tricks since she's been at it so long," offered another mother. "Miss Betty has seen it all."

While visiting, Mom glanced up and saw Jason swimming laps, Katie blowing bubbles in the water, and Benny hanging on to the edge in the pool. Mom thought to herself how she could never instruct nine children in the pool at all different levels. The woman was super human. Sharon, the helper, just watched to make sure that no one drowned.

Soon the hour was up, and it was time to get out of the pool.

"See you tomorrow, gang. I've got another class coming, so hop to it," said Miss Betty in her gravelly voice.

"Mom, I'm whooped." Jason sighed as

he slowly climbed into the van like his feet were made of lead. "Do I have to go back tomorrow?"

"Of course you do. This is how you build on your skills," Mom said.

"But, Mom, didn't you see me? All I did was swim laps, and I hardly got to play," Jason complained as his voice began to tremble. "My chest hurts from swimming so much. She's too tough on me."

"Okay. It's all right. Let's just go home and relax a bit," said Mom.

Katie chattered all of the way home about her two new friends she made while Benny continued to comment on Miss Betty's wild hair and scratchy voice.

As the next morning rolled around, the Jaspers were getting ready to head back to swim lessons.

# Meet the Jaspers

"Mommy, where is my *Bomhamas* swim-suit?" Ben called from his bedroom.

"Your *Bomhamas* suit is hanging in the bathroom on the back of the door," Mom answered.

It was just as easy to talk like Ben since everyone knew he was referring to his blue-and-orange Hawaiian-print swim trunks. He was trying to say *Bahamas*, which is an island in the Caribbean Sea.

"I need *gobbles* too. My eyes are itchy."

No one took the time to figure out why he said *Bomhamas* and *gobbles* instead of *komhamas* and *koggles*.

"Okay, sweetie. I'm putting them in the swimming bag as we speak," Mom said.

"Mom, do I really have to go to swim-ming lessons anymore? It's too hard for me," Jason said as his eyes were ready to spill over with tears. "The highest group is too tough."

"Who else is in your group?" asked Mom.

"Just Maddie, and she's thirteen. She said she was going to try out for the swim team," Jason replied.

"Well, let's get going so I can talk to Miss Betty before class starts and see if we can work something out," Mom said.

As they drove up, Mom jumped out of the van quickly so she could catch Miss Betty alone.

"Uh, Betty, could I talk to you for a minute?" Mom asked.

"Sure, hon. What's up?" questioned Miss Betty.

"I hate to ask, but do you think you could put Jason in the group below the one he's in now? He seems to be feeling a little overwhelmed with so much lap swimming," Mom timidly asked of her former instructor.

"Now, Susan, he's a nice, big, teenage

boy. He should be fine swimming all those laps," said Miss Betty.

"No, ma'am. He's only nine and going into the fourth grade in the fall. He's just the size of a thirteen-year-old. He's big for his age. He's only had lessons at the city pool for three years now," Mom gushed.

"Oh, darling, he just acted so grown-up. Well, we'll fix that right up in a jiffy. He can be with Joe in the middle group instead. How's that?" Miss Betty offered.

"That would be great. Won't that be great, Jason? That'll be great," responded Mom, still feeling a little flustered from having to confront her former teacher. "Don't forget your *gobbles*, Ben," Mom added quickly.

All nine kids were back in the pool. This time, Ben sat right away on the edge of the pool and dangled his legs in. Miss Betty patted her hand on the side of the pool and asked Ben to come over by her, and he did. Before long, Ben was joining in with his group and bobbing for apples to practice blowing out air underwater.

"We'll drown-proof you yet, Benjamin Jasper," said Miss Betty.

"Yes, ma'am," said Ben.

"Ben, why don't you dip your face in the water and grab this ring?" asked Miss Betty.

"Yes, ma'am," said Ben. He retrieved the red ring. "Do you want me to get the blue one too?"

"Sure," said Miss Betty.

It was farther and deeper. Ben took a breath and plunged himself under the water and began to reach his arms for the blue ring and got it.

"Way to go, Ben. I think you're a natural, and you already know your colors."

Ben kept practicing holding his breath and paddling underwater. He was swimming.

# Meet the Jaspers

"I might have to put you in Katie's group if you keep this up," Miss Betty said with her raspy voice.

"Miss Betty, can I touch your hair?" Ben asked as he reached for her long, black, wet, frizzy locks.

"Sure. Can I touch yours?" Miss Betty asked as she reached for the main cowlick in the center of Ben's forehead.

"Why is your voice so scratchy?" Ben inquired.

"Well, I'm pretty old, you know, and I spend so much time outside in this chlorine pool. I have allergies, and they make my voice sound like that," explained Miss Betty.

"I have allergies too," said Ben.

"I guess we have a few things in common, don't we?" said Miss Betty.

"Yes, ma'am," said Ben.

"Now, let's get cracking. Why don't you find me the orange ring now," Miss Betty asked.

Meanwhile, Jason and Joe were working on their strokes by holding on to the side of the pool. Katie was practicing diving off the side of the pool through an inner tube that the teacher was holding.

That day, all of the groups learned about what to do in a water emergency and how to make good decisions without panicking. Katie thought it was kind of scary. Miss Betty said they would be better prepared if they practiced what to do in dangerous water.

It was a full session, and they were tired by the time the lesson was over.

"How was it today, kids?" Mom asked in the van on the ride back home.

"Way better, Mom. Thanks for getting me in the right group," Jason gratefully said.

"I'm glad I could help," offered Mom. "How about Ben and Katie?"

"It was fun. I like diving through the inner tube," said Katie.

"I saw you, Katie. You looked like you were having fun," Mom said. "Ben, you looked pretty happy too. I saw you swimming underwater for the rings. Way to go. You all did great."

Soon, Friday rolled around after having lessons all week.

"Is this really our last day of seeing Miss Betty?" Katie asked. "She is such a nice teacher."

"I like her. She let me touch her hair. She's got allergies," offered Ben.

"It sounds like you learned a lot," said Mom, "*and* you learned to swim."

"What does that mean, Mom?" asked Katie.

"Well, you've heard of 'Don't judge a book by its cover'? It's best to get to know someone before you decide to like them or not. Once you got to know Miss Betty, you could see that she's not scary at all. Sometimes the best books have covers that are torn and well used. That's because it was a great book and everyone wanted to read it over and over," said Mom.

"Mommy, can I make Miss Betty a card before we go to lessons?" asked Katie, who loved to cut, color, tape, glue, or draw just about anything.

"I think that's a great idea, and I know she'll love it," said Mom.

Once they arrived at the last lesson that Friday, they poured out of the van, running toward the pool where Miss Betty waited. Benny and Katie gave her a big hug while Jason said hello.

What a great week. They had all learned so many new things and had a chance to practice them.

"Now I'm going to give you each a chance to jump off my diving board in the deep end if you want to since it's the last day. Do I have any volunteers?" asked Miss Betty.

Five of the nine children put their hands up. Ben saw that his brother and sister were willing, so his hand shot up and made six. The other three children from Ben's group didn't feel ready yet.

They lined up and took their turn. Miss Betty waited nearby in the deep end, floating on a noodle in case anybody needed help.

"Miss Betty, can I get my *gobbles* please?" Benny asked politely.

"Yes, Ben," answered Miss Betty.

First Maddie, the oldest, gracefully dove into the water, hardly making a splash at all. Then it was Jason's turn. He took a running leap and spread-eagled his arms and legs out and made a huge smacking sound as his belly slapped the surface of the water. He climbed out of the water with a big smile on his face. The other kids complimented him on his ability to splash so much water. Soon, it was Katie's turn.

"I would like to do a pencil dive. Is that okay?" Katie asked before she jumped straight off the end, feet first, with her legs and arms straight like a pencil.

Ben's turn finally came as he adjusted his goggles.

"Aah. *Geromino!*" Ben called as he dove off the end of the board as if he had been doing it all of his three and half years of life.

*What does Susan feed that kid?* Miss Betty thought to herself.

"Miss Betty, I have a card for you," Katie said as she handed over the slightly dripping handmade card consisting of old pieces of wrapping paper glued to a small piece of cardboard and popsicle sticks.

"Thank you, Katie. This is just precious," said Miss Betty, "And thanks for

# Meet the Jaspers

coming. Should I add your names to next year's permanent list?"

"Yes, that would be great. Thanks so much," said Mom.

"I think you learned a lot," Miss Betty said as the Jaspers all hugged her good-bye.

"Yes, ma'am," said Ben. "I learned how to swim, dive, and how to judge a book."

# Beauty Shop Bonanza

As the first day of school drew nearer, it was time for Katie to get her beauty-shop haircut. That way she would be all ready for first grade. Katie's mom had handled her haircuts until now. As a special treat, she was going to see Pam at Super Scissors Salon. Katie could hardly contain herself as she had talked about going to the hair salon nonstop. Katie had coerced Mom into making the appointment so she could have a "morning of beauty." Katie had been growing out her blonde bangs, which were now down to her chin. It was a painful process that required barrettes and headbands so her bangs wouldn't hang in her eyes. She had finally worn her mom down and convinced her to get her long hair cut to shoulder length.

"Mom, is it time to go yet?" asked Katie. "We don't want to be late for Pam." Katie appeared in a pink flowered sundress and orange flip flops. She was carrying her mother's old purse that contained Katie's hairbrush and lip gloss.

"Not quite yet, sweetie," replied Mom. "We'll leave in ten minutes."

"Do we have to go too?" asked Jason.

"Yes, Jason, you have to go too," Mom answered. "I need you to come with me and help entertain your brother."

"When will I be old enough to stay

home alone, Mom? Don't you trust me?" inquired Jason.

"It's not that I don't trust you, Jason. You see, there is this thing called good judgment, and it is against my good judgment to leave my nine-year-old son home alone. When you're closer to twelve, we could let you stay home alone," Mom said with a smile growing on her face. "Then you'll be old enough to take the babysitting class. That way you could keep Katie and Benny home alone with you while I get groceries or run other errands," Mom offered.

"Sheesh," complained Jason. "I don't know which is worse. Going with all of you or staying home with them."

"Well, don't worry about it since you have a few more years for that to happen," said Mom. "Besides, it's time to go."

It was a gray and rainy morning as they drove to Super Scissors.

"Did you bring an umbrella, Mom?" asked Katie. "I don't want to get my new hairdo wet when we come out of the salon."

"I think I should be able to find one in here somewhere. We have everything else you could imagine. Why not an umbrella?" Mom kidded as she dug through an old backpack with snack crackers, a toy fire truck, three broken crayons, and a torn coloring book. "Voila. This might not be the cleanest van in the neighborhood, but when you need something, you can usually find it in here."

Katie was bubbling with excitement as they entered Super Scissors and were greeted by Pam. She said she would be right with them. Katie began to leaf through some of the hair magazines on the table. She felt so grown up sitting in the waiting area with her legs crossed and licking her fingers to help her turn the pages. Katie noticed some pretty unusual hairstyles and wondered if her mom would ever let her have her hair done so uneven and multicolored like that.

"So, Katie, what are we going to do for you today?" asked Pam.

"Give me the works. This is my morning of beauty, after all," said Katie.

"How about cutting it about up to here?" Mom motioned to her shoulders with her hands. "Are you really sure, Katie? That's about six inches of beautiful blonde hair that we're talking about."

"Yes, Mom, I'm sure," Katie replied as she climbed up into the shampoo chair just like she had been doing it all of her life.

Katie was thoroughly enjoying getting her hair shampooed and conditioned. Pam began to quiz Katie about her friends and summer vacation.

Benny and Jason sat in the chairs in the waiting area. Jason brought a book to read, and Benny played with the fire truck. He drove it around the waiting area, making siren noises and spitting motor sounds.

Katie now had her hair wrapped up in a towel as she made her way to the haircut chair. Katie got to go for a small ride as Pam adjusted the chair to the right height.

"I want a ride," said Benny.

"When I'm done with your sister I'll let you have a ride, okay?" offered Pam thoughtfully.

"Okay," Ben said as he walked nearer to get a closer look at Katie's hair falling to the floor in big chunks. "Look at your hair, Katie. Are you going to be bald like Grandpa?"

"No," Katie answered. "It's just going to be at my shoulders so it can catch up with my bangs faster."

"That's quite a cowlick you have there," Pam noticed upon closer inspection of Ben's bangs.

"I've been meaning to ask you about

that," Mom said. "The barber said that there isn't much that can be done for it. A cowlick is just something that you have to live with, and the barber counted seven. Is that true?"

"Well, yes and no," Pam answered. "It depends on how you cut it to help it lay flat. It will *never* go away though."

"Never ever?" Ben said as he rubbed his hair. "I don't want it to last forever."

"Maybe your Mom could make you an appointment sometime and I could try to cut it to help it lie down flatter on your head," offered Pam.

"Would you do that for me?" asked Benny.

"Yes, I would," answered Pam with a smile.

"My barber can't make it go down," Ben said as he tried to rub his bangs flat.

Pam began to blow dry Katie's hair. Ben covered his ears and pranced around the salon with his legs bouncing from side to side as he was trying to escape from the noise of the loud hairdryer.

"So what do you think?" Pam asked.

"I love it," Katie said with a toothless smile erupting on her face. She turned her head and felt her hair swing back and forth on her shoulders. "Can I come here for all of my haircuts, Mom?"

"That would be fun, wouldn't it?" answered Mom. "It really is pretty, Katie. Thanks, Pam."

"Can I have my ride now?" Ben asked with a big charming smile.

"Of course you can. I nearly forgot," Pam said as Ben climbed in the chair and got raised up and lowered down. He even got spun around twice. "Thanks for coming," Pam said as they all said good-bye. Pam rubbed Ben's bangs one more time as if she couldn't help herself from trying to hold the cowlicks down.

# Meet the Jaspers

The Jasper children had a big afternoon planned on Gardener Loop since they only had a few more weeks of summer vacation left. The rain had let up, and it turned out to be a warm, sunny afternoon.

"We really have to make every moment count," Jason said to Katie. "Let's think of something fun to do."

Jason realized he had to rely on Katie and Ben for entertainment, as the usual bunch of neighborhood kids were not home. This left the Jasper children to come up with their own activity for the afternoon. Then, suddenly, Jason had a great idea.

"Let's make a buried treasure!" Jason excitedly shared his big thought.

"What's that?" Ben asked curiously.

"That's when you gather up stuff, put it in a container, and then you bury it," Jason answered.

"Why do we want to bury a treasure?"

Katie asked, still swinging her shoulder-length hair and notching her hip.

"Because it will be fun. Besides, Mom won't let us watch any more TV this afternoon," answered Jason excitedly. "We'll need to gather things up that we want to put in the buried treasure. You probably don't want to pick anything too valuable in case we can't find it when we want to dig it up."

"I'm getting a great idea already," Katie called as she ran off to her bedroom.

Meanwhile, Jason was trying to convince his mother by asking, "Can I please scrape out the creamy peanut butter container. It's almost empty. Since the jar is plastic, it's much safer to bury than glass."

"Sure. As long as you save the peanut butter. We don't want to waste food. Oh, and wash the jar too."

Ten minutes later, Jason had the jar ready, and Katie came down with two stick-on tattoos from the Sugar O's cereal box. She also found a small, pink bouncy ball to go with four small silver jacks and a tube of yellow lipstick that she didn't really care for. Benny brought down a green army man with an arm missing and a green Slick Wheels race car with only three tires on it.

"Good job, people," Jason said seriously as he held his hands behind his back. He took on the usual role as leader of the trio. "You picked some old, broken junk, but you followed my directions exactly. You didn't gather anything too valuable."

Jason revealed his treasures to the others. He had put in a blue glittery yo-yo minus the string. He also found a space-shuttle eraser and a moon-shaped nightlight that didn't work anymore. They put their items in the jar and screwed the lid on tight.

The Jasper children set off through the backyard and climbed the fence into the cow pasture that was behind their neighborhood. Woody stood at the fence and barked, asking to come with them.

"Sorry, Woody," said Jason. "You can't come on this mission. We're heading for the cow pasture."

Even though the Jaspers lived in a neighborhood on a quiet street, there was a cow pasture where black-and-white Holsteins grazed, behind their backyard. The cows were their backyard neighbors.

"Now, there are several elements of danger here on our mission. Katie and Ben, it is your job to be on the lookout for any enemy activity," ordered Jason. "Also watch your step for cow pies."

"Who's the enemy?" asked Katie

"The cows, silly. We just don't want to make them mad. This is their field, after all," said Jason. "Now, I'm going to count off one hundred and one paces straight ahead, and that's where we'll dig a hole and bury the treasure. Here, Ben. You carry the shovel."

It was big and heavy, but Ben took his task of shovel holder very seriously.

"How much farther?" Katie asked as she was nervously looking for any cattle to come charging at them.

"Seventy-eight, seventy-nine," Jason stopped impatiently. "Don't interrupt your commander in the middle of the mission or we might have to start all over."

"Sorry," Katie apologized as she saw a monarch butterfly fluttering through the pasture. "Why are you talking like that anyway?"

"Because that's how army leaders talk. At least the ones I've seen on TV. Okay. Here we are at one hundred and one paces. Let's start digging," Jason ordered.

The dirt was softened by the rain but

still was hard to dig. By taking turns, they were able to dig twelve inches down. They put the plastic peanut butter jar in the shallow hole and began to cover it up.

"How will we find our buried treasure?" asked Katie, thinking that the yellow lipstick might still come in handy sometime.

"That's true. We should draw a map showing how to get to this spot," offered Jason.

"Maybe we should mark the spot with something so we'll know how to find our treasure," Katie suggested.

"We can't do that. It could compromise the treasure's location to the enemy," said Jason.

"Cows aren't that smart, are they?" asked Katie

"Well, there could be other enemies out there," said Jason. "We better get out of this location before we are seen."

They ran together back through the pasture, over the fence, and back into the safety of their own backyard. They collapsed out of breath under the apple tree as beads of sweat were running down their faces.

"That was scary," said Ben, with round, honest eyes.

"And tiring," added Katie. "When will we go find our buried treasure?"

"The fun part is to wait a while so that it's a little bit hard to find," answered Jason. "All right troops. Dismissed."

"I need a break, Jason. You worked us hard," Katie offered with her cheeks still rosy.

"I'm *kesausted*," said Ben. "Let's go in."

Later that evening, Katie and Jason were telling Dad about their big day. Katie jabbered on about her trip to Super Scissors, and Jason told about the buried treasure.

"Where is Ben, by the way?" asked Dad.

"He's still brushing his teeth, I guess," Jason offered.

"Katie, why don't you run to the bathroom and tell Ben that Daddy said to hurry up. I want to hear about his day," Dad said.

Katie obediently took off ready to tell her little brother what to do.

"Daddy! Come quick!" Katie called. "It's an emergency!"

Dad sped up the stairs, his head spinning and his stomach churning. What kind of poison had Ben gotten into? Maybe he cut himself with a razor? The terrible thoughts were limitless.

"Daddy, Ben cut his hair!" Katie said with alarm and pointing at her younger brother. "Look."

Dad looked relieved when he saw Ben sitting upright in the empty tub with his pajamas on and no blood anywhere. There were small tufts of hair all over the tub.

"Benny, what are you doing?" Dad asked.

"I was trying to fix my cowlick," whimpered Ben with his head held down. Ben

was still holding scissors in his hand and was unable to look his dad in the eye. His hair looked normal except for the front of his head. He had cut his bangs off to the scalp.

"Son, I know you don't like your cowlick, but cutting it off won't make it go away," explained Dad. "Jason, run and find your mother, but don't scare her. Just tell her that I need to see her."

"The hair lady said she could fix it. I made it go away," said Ben with an ashamed voice. Katie helpfully held up a mirror in front of Ben's face so he could see his new reflection. He began to cry.

"Oh my." Mom gasped as she entered the upstairs bathroom. She could see immediately the one thing missing on the front of her little boy's forehead. She held back a giggle as she put her hand in front of her face. "It's okay, honey. We'll see if we can do something to fix it," Mom soothed as she hugged Ben tight.

"Katie and Jason, why don't you go to your rooms and start reading. This bathroom is too small for all five of us," Dad offered.

"You know the only cure is to buzz off his whole head of hair, don't you?" whispered Mom.

"I figured as much," Dad responded. "It's too late now to do anything about it tonight though. Let's just put them to bed and take care of it tomorrow."

"Good idea. I'll call Pam in the morning and see if she can help us out," offered Mom.

The next morning was a beautiful Saturday without a cloud in the blue sky. Dad sped along the street as he took Ben to Super Scissors. Jason and Katie went school clothes shopping with Mom.

"Thanks for squeezing us in early like this, Pam," Dad said appreciatively. "As you can see, we're in a bit of a bad way."

"Climb on up here, Ben. Just like yesterday," said Pam.

She had a booster seat to fit on top of the chair, and she covered Ben in a plastic cape with teddy bears on it.

"Now, sit real still for Mr. Buzz Buzz, my clippers, and you can have a lollipop when I'm all done."

"How are you going to fix my cowlick?" asked Ben.

"Well, this isn't the way that I had planned, but this will take care of it for a little while. When it grows back in, it will stick up again," Pam said with a little smile. "When your cowlick does grow back, come and see me and I'll use my special scissors to thin out your bangs to help it lie down a little flatter."

# Meet the Jaspers

Pam proceeded to start the clippers and ran them back and forth over his entire head. She had to cut off all of his hair to make it even with the haircut from the night before. He had about a quarter of an inch of hair left on his head when it was all said and done.

"My hair is all gone," whimpered Ben. "Now I look bald like Grandpa."

"Hair grows back, Ben," encouraged Dad. "And remember"—Dad pointed at the framed certificate on the wall of the salon—"only grownups and people with a hair-cutting license are allowed to cut your hair."

"Okay. Pam really did fix my cowlick," Ben said as he tried to cheer himself up. "Can I have a ride in the chair again?" After he spun around, he was off and running with his new haircut, minus the cowlick, at least for a little while anyway.

# Super Special Visitors

It was one of the best times of the year. Grandma and Grandpa Jasper were coming to visit for a week before school started. It was almost time for their plane to arrive at the small airport near Clearyville. They were coming all the way from Texas, and the Jasper children could hardly contain their excitement.

"I think I see their plane," said Jason.

"Where?" Dad asked as Jason pointed to the sky. Dad was excited too since he hadn't seen his parents since last summer.

Before they knew it, the plane had landed and let its passengers off. Out came Grandma and Grandpa Jasper from the hallway. They had big, circling hugs for everyone.

"You are all such a sight for sore eyes," Grandma Jasper said.

"Oh, it's been too long." said Grandpa Jasper. "I think all of you kids have grown at least a foot since last summer."

"They are growing like weeds," Dad offered.

"What do you feed these kids?" Grandpa Jasper asked.

"Lots. It seems that the kitchen is always open. They get outside and play in the fresh air too. Right, guys?" Mom asked.

"Well, let's get your bags picked up and

get on home," said Dad. "You must be tired from the big day."

"Yep. Our day started at four thirty this morning, Texas time, just so we could fly here and see our kids," said Grandpa in a big, booming voice while he reached for another hug.

Grandma and Grandpa Jasper had moved to Texas from Michigan when the snowy winters got too cold.

"Susan's got a delicious spaghetti sauce simmering in the crock pot," said Dad.

"Well, I wanted to have something waiting for us to eat in case the plane was late or something." Mom blushed as she explained.

"Oh, that sounds delicious," said Grandma. "You know we're starving since we didn't eat on the airplane."

Everyone took turns unloading the van and helped Grandma and Grandpa settle into Jason's room. He had the biggest bed and the most space for company. Jason would have to sleep on the top bunk in Ben's room. The top bunk was fun, but Ben wiggled and rolled over half the night, shaking the bed. Ben also talked in his sleep. Jason would make the best of it because Grandma and Grandpa were here.

The smell of spaghetti sauce and garlic bread erupted from the Jaspers' kitchen as they all settled down to a delicious meal.

"I love your new haircut, Katie," Grandma complimented. "You look so grown-up and ready to be a first-grader."

"Thanks, Grandma. I am going to be a *grader* now that I'm not in kindergarten anymore," Katie commented.

Grandma Jasper had a puzzled look on her face.

"You know, Grandma, first-grader, second-grader, all the way to a twelfth-grader."

# Meet the Jaspers

"Oh, I see Katie. You are going to be a *grader* now," Grandma realized.

"We like your new haircut too, Ben," Grandpa quickly offered as he rubbed Ben's buzz cut with his big hand.

"Thanks," said Ben as he touched where his bangs used to be. "I got rid of my cowlick."

"Yes, I see that you did," Grandpa said as he tried not to smile.

"We sure appreciate you coming," said Mom. "I'm sorry about the yard sale that we're having this weekend, but it'll be such a big help having you here to watch the kids while we're busy with the customers."

"No problem, Susan," soothed Grandma Jasper. "We're just so glad to be here at a time when we can help you out."

The family had been very busy preparing for Grandma and Grandpa Jasper's visit. Katie always noticed how much cleaning happened when company was coming. Mom told Katie

that she always liked to have the house looking nice for Grandma and Grandpa when
they arrived. While Mom was cleaning, she
kept finding things that needed to be sorted
through and gotten rid of. An annual yard
sale was a logical way for the Jaspers to keep
their household in order.

The next two days, Mom kept on gathering, sorting, and price-tagging all of their
unwanted treasures while Grandma and
Grandpa took the kids to the playground
with ice cream treats afterward. The Jasper
children always had so much fun when they
came to visit. Katie loved the extra-special
attention. Grandma could read extra stories
and play games. Grandpa loved to build with
blocks and play trains. The Jaspers loved having Grandma and Grandpa come to visit.

When Saturday morning arrived, Mom
awoke at 6:00 a.m. to be prepared to greet
the hardcore yard sale shoppers.

# Meet the Jaspers

Mom busied herself with the final yard sale organization. Shoppers began to arrive. Soon Dad emerged from the house, holding Benny in his arms.

"Someone wanted to say good morning to his Mommy," Dad said as he held Ben out for a hug and kiss from his mother.

"I just needed to hug you," Ben said as Mom realized that she'd better pay attention to the next sale.

"Thank you for the nice hug, sweetie. Why don't you go in with Grandma and Grandpa and Daddy can help me out here for a little while," said Mom as Benny pattered off into the house in his racecar pajamas. Dad and Mom stayed very busy working the sale.

As the morning progressed, the Jasper children came up with the idea to have a lemonade stand.

"Shoppers get thirsty," Jason said. "We could sell them a glass of lemonade, and maybe they'd feel so good that they'll buy more stuff."

"I'll get paper and markers to make a sign," offered Katie.

They busied themselves with gathering the supplies, making lemonade, and making signs. Grandma helped them get set up near the front porch. Their sign read:

Ice Cold Lemonade- 25 cents
2 glasses- 50 cents
3 glasses- $1.00

Grandma hated to point out that they weren't giving their customers much of a break for buying three lemonades. The lemonade stand kept them entertained.

"I hope we make lots of money on our lemonade stand," Katie said excitedly. "I'm saving up for a Barbie alarm clock. That way I can wake up for school all by myself."

"I could use a new puck for street hockey," Jason said. "Having your own business is pretty cool." Jason looked across the garage at an old piece of furniture with a look of shock and disappointment on his face.

"Why are you selling the black recliner, Mom?" asked Jason. "It's perfectly good."

"I know you love that chair, Jason," Mom said as she distastefully looked at the black imitation leather recliner.

That chair had been a fixture in their basement for as long as Jason could remember.

"I would like to fix up the basement into a play room and needed to make some space."

"I'll just miss it. That's all," Jason said sentimentally. "It was a good chair."

"Well, who knows," Mom offered. "It might not sell anyway. But if we get enough money from the yard sale, maybe we could get an air hockey table for our new play room in the basement."

"Sweet, Mom. That's a pretty cool idea," Jason said, changing his mind about the chair.

This prompted all of the Jasper children to take turns sitting in the black recliner and speaking to it. Benny rubbed the arm of the chair and patted the headrest with his hand. They wanted to thank it for being such a nice chair. Grandma even sat in the chair.

"What's that book, Grandma?" Katie asked as she noticed Grandma with a pretty aqua book with flowers on it.

"Well, this special book is my memory journal. I keep picking it up and writing in it. I want to remember and share with my grandchildren all of the wonderful things that I got to do as a child and in the past," Grandma explained.

Katie began to look at it too.

"I love this book, Grandma," said Katie. "It's so pretty, but what does it say? I can't read your loopy letters."

"I've just been writing down special memories that I have about my own childhood and raising your dad and your aunties. I thought you all might enjoy it someday."

"What a lovely idea," Mom said as she walked over since there was a lull with the shoppers. "You're so thoughtful to think of such a thing. I'll have to ask my own mother to make one."

"Well, I have thoroughly enjoyed thinking through all of the memories and putting them down on paper," said Grandma. "We'll have to take a look at it after the sale today. Why don't I make lunch for everyone, and we'll bring you out a sandwich, Susan?"

"That would be so great," said Mom.

Little by little, items sold and the piles

on the tables got smaller and smaller. Jason stayed to help Mom move things around so that the customers could see everything.

Finally, an interested shopper asked about the recliner in the driveway. He examined the chair closely and sat in it to see how he fit in the chair. The sticker was marked $20.

"Could I take it off your hands for ten dollars?" asked the thin, gray-haired man. "That's about the best I can do. It's for my grandson. He just got out of the hospital last week. Maybe you read about his truck accident over on Webster Road in the newspaper?"

"Yes, we did read about an accident there," Mom said as she recalled pictures of a bad truck accident. "I'm so glad he's home from the hospital. Will he be okay?"

"The doctors say he'll be fine. Complete recovery," replied the man.

"That's such good news. The chair is in great condition," said Mom. "How about eleven dollars, and you've got yourself a twen-ty-five-year-old fake leather recliner?" Mom couldn't seem to stop negotiating prices, even when she could see someone truly in need.

"I'll take it," the man said with a smile. Mom was just happy she wouldn't have to move it back into the garage or donate it to the thrift shop.

"Good-bye, chair," Ben said to the piece of furniture.

"Good times." Jason sighed as he brushed his hand across the chair one last time before the recliner was loaded into the back of the truck. The man's vehicle was al-ready overflowing with other yard-sale pur-chases from earlier that day.

Soon the sale was over, and the Jaspers began to box up things to donate to the thrift store while they made another to give to the church nursery. Mom happily counted the contents of the money box, realizing that the air hockey table would become a reality for the Jasper children.

Thankfully, Grandma had prepared her own homemade fried chicken with mashed potatoes and gravy so that the whole family could sit down to share a delicious meal together. This had been a busy day of running the yard sale and operating the lemonade stand.

"Grandma, why don't you read us a story from that book you were writing in today?" asked Katie once the dishes were cleared and the leftovers were put away.

"Well, let me go get it," said Grandma. "In fact, why don't you run and get it for me, Katie? It should be on the dresser in Jason's room.

Katie came back a few minutes later. "I can't find it, Grandma," said Katie.

"Well, I'll just have to go look then, won't I?" Grandma Jasper said with a cheerful smile.

Ben climbed up into his Grandpa Jasper's lap, which was one of his favorite places to sit.

"Well, I can't seem to find the book upstairs," Grandma Jasper said when she returned. "Maybe we left it in the garage accidentally when we were outside."

The Jaspers searched high and low, but, unfortunately, they couldn't find the memory book anywhere. Grandma was now upset.

"I don't know what could have happened to the book," she said. "It's just that I've put so much time into writing about my memories. I would hate to lose it."

They kept on searching under beds and in book shelves, inside cupboards, and in closets.

"Dad, you always tell me to go back to

where I was when I last saw the missing thing," said Jason. "When did you last see your memory book, Grandma?"

"Well, I know that we were looking at it outside in that old chair, and then I came in to make lunch. I'm just sure that I took it upstairs," Grandma Jasper worriedly answered.

"Could it be stuck in the old, black recliner somewhere, Mom?" Katie's dad asked. "We have searched everywhere."

"I suppose anything is possible," replied Grandma. "But that means it's gone with the man in that truck full of stuff. How will we ever figure out who that man was?"

"Maybe we could run an ad in the newspaper, asking for the man who bought our chair to call us," Dad suggested.

"That's it!" shouted Mom excitedly. "The newspaper! The man said that his grandson was just in a car accident, and the story was in the paper. I remember seeing the picture. Now we just need to find the newspaper and we'll see the name. Then we can find the man with our chair." Mom became more excited the more she talked.

Sometimes Katie wondered if her mother remembered to breathe.

Mom ran to the recycling bin in the garage with Jason, and they began searching through last week's newspapers, hoping they would find the article. Jason found it in last Wednesday's paper.

"Isn't it great, Mom, that I forgot to take out the newspaper recycling to the curb?" Jason asked.

"This time, but let's not make a habit of it. Okay?" Mom answered.

Jason began to read aloud, "Travis Palmer escaped the rollover truck accident with a broken leg and other minor injuries Tuesday night. He was transported to

# Meet the Jaspers

Clearyville Regional Medical Center. I'll get the phone book."

Mom dialed. "Hi. Is Travis there?" Mom asked.

"This is," replied the voice.

"Hi there. This is Susan Jasper. Your grandpa just bought a black recliner from us today at our yard sale."

"Yeah. Thanks," said Travis. "It's just what I needed to elevate my leg."

"This is going to sound strange," Mom asked, "but could you reach your hand down in between the cushions and see if there is a book inside the chair?"

"Sure," said Travis, sounding a bit confused. "It'll take me a minute since I'm still using crutches."

"Yes, we were glad to hear that you are doing okay and came home from the hospital," said Mom after she realized she didn't even ask how he was feeling. While

121

she waited for him to check, she wondered where her manners had disappeared to.

"Yes, it's here! I've got the book," said Travis. "I also found forty-three cents, a baseball card, and an old lollipop stick. Would you like that too?"

"Oh, Travis. You're the best," said Mom. "If you wouldn't mind giving me your address, we'll be right over to pick up the book. It belongs to my husband's mother. Keep the change, and then the chair will only cost you ten fifty-seven," Mom said as she did the quick mental math.

"Well, we solved the mystery of the missing memory book," said Jason.

"Thank you so much," Grandma gushed. "I feel so silly for causing all of this fuss."

"We're just glad we were able to find it," said Dad as he headed out the door with Grandpa to pick up the memory book.

"Grandma, could you tell us a story from

your book about what it was like in the olden days?" Katie asked. "You know, when life was in black and white."

"Sure," Grandma answered, "but you know that only the pictures were black and white. We lived in beautiful color just like we do today."

"How about just one story tonight and then it's bedtime," Mom suggested.

"Now let me think of an interesting story. Oh yes, but it's a story of a time that I told a little lie. Are you ready?" Grandma began. "Back when I was ten and my little brother Robby was eight—that's your great-uncle Bob, by the way—my dad had to milk the cows every day and we had to chase the cattle back to the barn after grazing all day out in the pasture. Well, Robby and I were following behind the cows, and in our bare feet no less. Your great grandma didn't mind if we went without shoes, except in the cow pasture. Well, sure enough, I stepped on a rusty nail, and oh boy did it hurt. The bad part was I knew that I had disobeyed my mom by going barefooted in the pasture, so I didn't tell her about the nail wound in my foot. Sure enough, it got infected, and I still didn't tell my mom. I let it go for three whole days without attention, and then I got really sick with blood poisoning. The doctor came and gave me medicine, and I had to be in bed for a week. Finally, I had to tell Great Grandma Ruth what I had done. Of course, she just wanted me to get better, but it could have all been avoided if I had just done what my mom knew was best. So those are just some words of wisdom from a wise old Grandma," said Grandma Jasper. You'll find that story and many others in my memory book."

"On that note, I think you should all obey *this* mother and go get ready for bed," Mom said with a smile.

# River Ride

Sadly, Grandma and Grandpa Jasper's week had come and gone. The Jaspers said their tearful good-byes at the airport. Katie waved to her grandparents through the big glass window.

"The week went so fast." Katie sniffed. "I miss Grandma and Grandpa already."

"I miss them too," agreed Jason. "When will we see them again?"

"We'll see them as soon as we can. I

know it's hard," consoled Dad. "I feel sad when they leave too. We'll just have to talk on the phone and send e-mails until our next visit."

"Besides, we have big plans for the next few days before school starts," Mom said as she exchanged a knowing look with Dad.

"What is it?" Jason asked.

"What is it?" Ben mimicked.

"I know what it is," Katie said as she giggled. "I have my soccer practice this afternoon. Right, Mom?"

"Oh, boy. I can hardly wait," Jason answered impatiently.

"Yes, Katie, your soccer practice is this afternoon, but we made some plans for tomorrow if the weather holds," Mom said.

The Jasper children's minds were racing, trying to guess what they were going to do.

"Are we camping again?" Katie asked. "Because that would be pretty fun."

# Meet the Jaspers

"Are we going fishing?" asked Ben.

"No," answered Dad. "But you will need your swimsuits."

"I know what it is!" yelled Jason excitedly. "Are we going tubing on the Pine River?"

"That's it," answered Dad. "We thought it would be fun since summer is almost over. We knew you could use a little something to look forward to after Grandma and Grandpa went back home."

"You guys are the best!" Jason said as he reached forward in the van to hug his Dad around the neck the best he could with his seatbelt on.

The Jasper children had been asking to ride inner tubes down the Pine River since last summer, but Ben had always been too little for them to go as a family. The Pine River was known for its shallow depths and slow, steady currents. It was spring fed, so the water was very clean and was a beautiful clear, green color. This was the perfect time to go, as the Michigan sun had all summer to warm the river to a comfortable temperature. The Jasper children could hardly contain their excitement as they began to plan their river ride.

"What swimsuit are you going to wear, Mom?" Katie asked. "I think I'll wear my two-piece orange-and-black one."

"Yeah, wear the orange *kikini*," Ben offered helpfully. "I like that one."

"The important thing is to be comfortable on the inner tube," Mom said. "I'll pack a lunch, and we'll be able to make a day of it."

"Let's get organized so we get a good start in the morning. We want to be there by eleven o'clock," Dad said. "But before we do that, we have to get Katie to her soccer practice. Are you excited, honey?"

"Yes!" Katie answered. "I've got two special things to look forward to."

"Why don't you get a snack and then

get dressed. It's almost time for practice," said Dad.

"Are you going to take me?" Katie asked.

"Since I'm still on vacation, I would love to take you, Katie," Dad said. "I think we'll take the boys with us too and give Mom a little break. That way she can get some groceries without everyone's help."

A few minutes later, Katie came down in her soccer clothes. She was fast, but she had lots of practice over the years. She had been dressing by herself even before her second birthday. Katie usually liked to change outfits at least three times a day. She did need help, however, pulling up the long soccer socks over the bulky shin guards that protected her legs from getting kicked.

"Where are your old *fleats,* Katie?" Ben asked as he was trying to pull on Jason's old pair of shin guards from a few years ago.

"What are you doing, Ben?" Katie asked

even though she already knew the answer. Ben thought he was going to have practice too. Why did he have to try to do everything that she did?

"I need *fleats* so I can run fast," said Ben in his gravelly voice.

"They're called cleats, and it's *my* practice!" argued Katie.

"I just want to play," answered Ben.

"Let me put your hair in a ponytail so it's not in your way, Katie," Dad said as he awkwardly twisted and pulled at his daughter's hair.

"Ouch, Daddy," Katie complained. "It doesn't hurt like that when Mom fixes it."

"That should do it," Dad said as he quickly stepped back from Katie's lopsided ponytail on the back of her head. There were loose hairs falling out all over. "Let's go or we'll be late," Dad said quickly before he had to do any more work on the ponytail.

# Meet the Jaspers

At the soccer fields, other teams were practicing too. They found Katie's coach, who was a friend of Mom.

"Hi, Carol," greeted Dad. "Are we all set?"

"I think so, Jim. How are you, Katie?" asked the coach.

"I'm fine, Mrs. Simpson," Katie answered. "Do I call you Coach Carol now?"

"You can if you like," Coach Carol answered. "It looks as if Ben is ready to play too."

"Can I play, Coach Carol?" asked Ben.

"I suppose you could just play along with us for today, Ben, since some of the other kids are still on vacation. You won't be able to play in the game though," Coach Carol said with a smile unable to resist Ben's charms.

"All right!" Ben said with a growly sound to his voice. "Good thing I wore my soccer clothes."

"I do want you to be careful of the mud here.

We've had a lot of rain lately, and it makes for a very messy soccer field," said Coach Carol.

"Can we go now?" Jason asked as he rolled his eyes at his two younger siblings. He still didn't understand why he had to come. It was one thing when it was his practice, but this was pure torture being dragged to Katie's practice. Now it looked like Ben's practice too.

"Jason, we need to stay here and watch the practice. Katie's too young to be left alone. Besides, I want to watch. I'm usually at work, and I don't always get the chance to see you guys practice, so this is special for me," said Dad. "Why don't you walk around the field and see if you can find any of your friends here. Maybe they're watching their brother or sister play too."

"Okay," Jason answered reluctantly as he climbed down off the bleachers.

Coach Carol was setting up orange plastic cones for the team to practice dribbling the soccer ball through while weaving in and out. Interestingly, Ben kept up with the older kids that were Katie's age.

While Coach Carol was preparing the next activity, Katie turned around and gave her friend Molly a great big bear hug.

"I missed you, Molly!" said Katie. "Look how strong I am," as Katie lifted Molly up off the grass.

Before long, all six children on the team were lifting each other up to see which one was the strongest.

"Okay, Panthers. Eyes on me!" Coach Carol called. "We're going to try a little scrimmage just to see where we are."

She began to move the children about the field into their proper positions. It seemed easier for Coach Carol to pick them up and move them rather than try to explain where to stand.

"Pay attention, Katie!" Dad called.

Katie got a real serious look on her face

as she pulled up her shin guards and looked for the soccer ball.

"Okay, Dad. I love you!" Katie yelled as she was preparing to kick the ball.

Suddenly, from nowhere, in flew a monarch butterfly.

"Oh, look at the pretty butterfly," Katie said as she was off and running trying to catch it. Soon all of the children were trying to catch the orange-and-black-winged insect.

"Listen up, Panthers!" called Coach Carol. "We can chase the butterflies after practice. Now let's try this again." They started to kick the ball toward the small portable goal. "Good job! That's the way!"

Ben really seemed to enjoy playing soccer. He also enjoyed kicking up the loose clumps of mud that were resting on the field. He could play nearly as well as Hannah and Joey. It was too bad that he was only three and a half and too young to play on the team. You had to be at least five to play in the Clearyville City League.

Before long, Molly and Katie were dancing and singing with each other in the middle of the field as the others were trying to scrimmage. The dancing was getting harder, though, as Katie noticed the mud was starting to collect on the bottom of her shoes. There must have been an inch and a half built up on the bottom of her cleats.

"Molly, look at my high heels I'm wearing," said Katie. "Do you like my platform shoes?"

"I do," answered Molly with a squeal. "Do you like mine?"

They began to compare to see who had the thickest clumps of mud stuck to the bottom of their cleats. Katie stood next to Molly by holding their feet side by side.

"Girls, over here. Let's get in the game," Coach Carol said.

"Come on, Katie," Dad said quietly to his

daughter as he walked toward her. "You came here to practice soccer, not have a dance party."

"I'm sorry, Dad," Katie said. "I was just so excited to see Molly." Katie ran to hug her dad's leg.

Ben saw the hug and stopped kicking the ball and ran for his dad too.

"I just need to hug you!" Ben announced as he threw his arms around his dad's neck. Ben started to run back to the scrimmage and stopped in his tracks. "When will it be snack time?"

"I think they just have snack on game day, Benny," Dad answered. "We'll be leaving shortly and having dinner at home."

"I think that about wraps it up for our first practice," Coach Carol said with a sweaty, tired smile.

"How do you do it, Carol?" asked Dad quietly. "I have a headache from watching them, and I didn't have to do anything."

# Meet the Jaspers

"It's like this every year," Coach Carol answered. "They'll get the hang of it. By the way, I really wish Ben could play with us all of the time. He's a real natural. It's too bad he has to wait two more seasons to play."

"Thanks, Carol," said Dad. "We'll see you next time. Come on, kids. Let's go find Jason, and get those muddy cleats off before you climb into the van. Why don't we see if we can help Mom bring in the groceries."

They headed home.

Before they knew it, it was the next morning and they were loading the van and on their way to the Pine River Inner Tube Launch. It was nearly an hour drive, and the best part was that the weather looked as if it was going to be perfect for them.

As they pulled in to the parking lot, Dad offered to go rent the tubes while they got

137

the rest of their stuff out and organized. Katie wondered if her dad could even see while he was trying to roll and carry two huge inner tubes, one medium and two small, on his arms.

"The man in the rental office reminded me to make sure and have you three wear your life vests. We all know how important it is to be safe in the water." Dad said. "He also said that there is an area down the river where there is a tube chute. It sounds like a big slide, so that should be fun."

The Jaspers carried their tubes down to the launch area of the pretty, green river.

"I'm scared," Katie whimpered.

"There's nothing to be afraid of, Katie," Jason said matter of factly. "You've got on your life vest, so that will keep you safe. You can't sink with it on."

"This river is known for being shallow. I've heard it's not more than four feet deep," Dad reassured. "But you can never be too careful. We have to stick together at all times. I have this rope to help hold our tubes together like a big floating raft."

Once Katie climbed into her tube and began to gently float down the river, she could see how much fun it was, and the fear lifted.

"So what do you guys think?" asked Mom. "Is this everything you had hoped it would be?"

They began to float by other families in their tubes. Katie could tell that some of the others looked like high school and college students.

"This is so sweet," Jason answered. "Thanks for bringing us."

"Yeah. Thanks," said Katie.

Before long, they heard a loud roaring noise off in the distance.

"What's that noise?" Benny asked as he turned his head to listen harder.

"That must be the tube chute," Dad concluded.

Within another minute, they passed a sign that said, "Tube Chute Ahead," that confirmed their idea.

"I don't know, Jim. It sounds awfully loud. It must be big," Mom commented with concern.

As they rounded the bend in the river, they could see where part of the river was blocked off to make a big, deep pool of water where the forty-foot slide would drop the tubers in the big rushing mass of water.

Katie saw Mom's eyes grow big.

"I think I'll take Katie and Benny with me and avoid the chute. How about you, Jason?" Mom asked.

"I definitely want to ride the tube chute," Jason said with an eager smile.

"Well, I'll go with Jason," said Dad as he began to untie the ropes that connected the tubes together.

Mom got out of the water and helped Katie and Ben climb out of the river. They carried their tubes down further from where the tube chute let out. As they prepared to get back in the water, they saw Jason and Dad whiz by and get spit out into the deep pool of rushing water. Katie could barely hear Jason's squeals of delight over the rushing sound of water as he was pushed out. Katie began to wriggle in her life vest. She noticed her armpit had a sore spot where her swim suit was rubbing. She quickly adjusted the life vest by unsnapping the fasteners to make it more comfortable. Mom got the tubes ready.

"This looks like a good place to put in past the chute," Mom said. "Kids, hold on to this metal bar here while you get in your tube. Then I can climb in. That way we can float together until we catch up with Dad and Jason. Be careful. I can feel the current pulling a bit."

Katie could feel the strong pull of the

current from the tube chute, but she held on like Mom told her to. Katie's muscles shook from the force of the water.

"Mommy, my muscles are hurting," Katie whimpered. She couldn't hold on, and her hands let go. Whoosh. The current had such a strong force where it was rushing in from the tube chute. It knocked Katie backward and dragged her upside down under the water. Her life vest was torn from her body where she left it unfastened. Katie's water shoes were pulled off as her sunglasses were ripped from her face. She fought her way to the surface. Deep under the black water, Katie was pulled as her mind raced. Where were Ben and Mom? She popped up above the water and took a huge gasp of air. She called for help as she tried to fight the current.

"Mom, Dad! Help!" Katie screamed. She gulped as she tried to tread water like Miss Betty had taught her. She looked for

# Meet the Jaspers

Mom. Panic was setting in. Her voice could not be heard over the roar of the water. It was impossible to tread water against the power of the strong current.

Dad could see Katie was in trouble from farther down the river, where he and Jason waited in the calmer water. Dad climbed out and ran back along the edge and then jumped back in. The raging current was just too powerful. Dad could not swim close enough to help.

Katie struggled near exhaustion. *Why didn't I listen to Dad when he said to leave my life jacket on? What if I never see them again? Please, God, help!* Katie thought a silent prayer. Katie suddenly felt her body relax as she realized the current was too strong for her to fight. The thoughts of re-laxing her body filled her mind. Once Katie stopped fighting the current and let it carry her, she actually felt less panicked. Katie let

**143**

her body be dragged to the calmer part of the water. Mom swam toward Katie in the gentle water and hugged her and kissed her. Katie went limp in her mother's arms. Her muscles hurt, and she began to cry while Mom held her.

"Shhh. It's all right. I'm here now," Mom soothed as she rubbed Katie's back.

Suddenly, Katie caught a glimpse of Ben still in his tube hanging on to the metal bar with all he had. He was crying, and a man was helping him out of the water. Katie could see Dad making his way toward her. Before she knew it, Dad was scooping her up in his arms safely. The man who pulled Ben out was walking him down the bank as he cried, pointing toward the rest of the Jaspers.

"Is everyone okay?" Dad asked. He continued to hold Katie and lifted up Benny as well. "Thank you so much for bringing our son to us," Dad said gratefully to the stranger.

"I'm just glad I could help," the man said. "He was hanging on for dear life to that metal bar while sitting in the tube. He's one strong kid."

"You told me to hold on to the metal bar," Ben obediently reported with a sniffle.

"I *drowned*," Katie cried. "I was under the water, and I couldn't get out."

"You didn't drown, sweetie. We're all right here together," Mom said as she hugged her children tightly even though she was still shaking.

Dad put his arms around his whole family in a big, circling hug and breathed a sigh of relief. Mom was still trying to figure out what just happened.

"I'm so sorry, kids," Mom said. "I was trying to keep you all safe by not going down the tube chute. I tried to do the right thing. I would never put you in danger on purpose."

"We know that, Mom," said Jason, seeing that his mother truly shaken for the first time in his life. "We're all okay."

"I feel terrible too," said Dad. "I should never have let you put the tubes in there. The current was so strong, flipped you off and pulled you under. That part of the water wasn't meant for folks to be swimming in, especially without a life vest. What happened to yours, Katie?"

"I'm okay," Katie said. "I only drowned for a little bit."

"I was so scared, Katie, because I couldn't get to you," Mom said. "How did your life vest come off?"

"I undid my life vest because it was scratching. I was still wearing it."

"Yes, but you must have it fastened tight for the life vest to work," Mom corrected. "I tried so hard to get to you." Mom stopped herself.

# Meet the Jaspers

"Were you stuck in the water too, Mommy?"

"Yes, I was. I went in after you and tried to swim to you. The current was too strong even for me. I haven't been that scared in a long time," answered Mom. "My heart was pounding, and my legs are still shaking. I hope I can climb out of the river," Mom said with a smile.

"You did that for me?" Katie asked, as her parents gave her another hug. Katie had stopped crying now and was trying to help her mother feel better. "I can't wait to tell Grandma on the phone."

"Why don't you let Mommy and Daddy tell them in our own way so we don't scare them," said Dad with a strange sort of smile. "Now you know what we need to do here, don't you, Jasper family?"

"Leave," said Katie with the first smile she had allowed.

"Oh no. That would be too easy," said

Dad. "We need to get back on our horse and ride."

"What horse?" Benny asked.

"What Dad means is we need to get back in the river and finish our river ride," Jason added helpfully.

"I don't think the tube chute is such a great idea, Jim," said Mom.

"No, not the chute," answered Dad quickly. "What I meant was, let's put the tubes in farther down the river, where it's back to the safe, calm current and shallow, green river water. I think we need to finish what we started, or we might have regrets about it someday."

"Okay," answered Mom. "I just need a few more minutes to make sure that my legs are all done shaking."

The Jaspers did just that. They gratefully got back in their tubes and finished their Pine River ride with calm water and relaxing family fun….together.

# Meet the Jaspers

After their peaceful ride home in the van, the Jaspers had a delicious and comforting meal of grilled cheese sandwiches and tomato soup. After dinner, they talked about what a fun summer it had been and all of the things that they had to be grateful for.

"We sure have done some cool stuff lately," Jason reflected. "We've been camping and fishing and tubing."

"We had swim lessons, and I got a new haircut," Katie added. "I'm so glad Grandma and Grandpa came too.

"I got a haircut too," said Ben. "And we saw a bear."

"Oh yeah," remembered Katie. "I got lost and found…. twice. Once in the woods and once in the river."

"I'm so grateful that we're all safe now and that we're here together," Mom said.

"How could one family have so many adventures?" Dad asked.

"That's because we're the Jaspers," Katie said excitedly.

"Hey, what about our buried treasure!" Ben reminded.

"That's right. We did forget about our buried treasure," Jason said. "I'll find the map. Ben, you can help me get the shovels." Jason began to organize his thoughts enthusiastically for another fun-filled mission.

"I'll go fill a water bottle," Katie offered excitedly. "Let's bring Woody this time for protection."

And off the Jaspers went into the pasture with their shovels dragging behind them.